NODDY IN TOYLAND

Noddy and
the Singing Bush

Collins

An Imprint of HarperCollinsPublishers

NODDY

CLOCKWORK MOUSE

BIG-EARS

MARTHA

TESSIE BEAR

GOBBO

MR PLOD

MASTER TUBBY BEAR

SLY

ONKEY

MR WOBBLY MAN

BUMPY DOG

It was a cloudy afternoon in Toyland . . .

Noddy hummed happily to himself as he polished his car.

"See how smart I'm making you!" he exclaimed.

"You'll shine so brightly, it won't matter that the sun's behind the clouds."

"Hello Noddy!" said Jumbo as he came plodding past. "Would you like to buy this old gramophone off me? I'd only want eight sixpences."

Noddy would have loved to have bought the gramophone, but he did not have enough money.

"Today I've only got three sixpences, but you could take it to Dinah Doll – she might sell it for you."

"I found this old gramophone in my attic," Jumbo told Dinah Doll. "You make it work by putting a record on it and then winding the handle."

Fortunately, Jumbo had a record with him. He had found that in his attic as well!

Dinah Doll wanted to hear what the record sounded like so she did exactly as Jumbo had instructed, winding the gramophone handle.

A strange, magical sort of music began to play.

"Oh, it's beautiful..." Dinah sighed.

The music made everyone happy and dreamy.
  They all twirled about, unable to stop themselves.
  Everyone who came to the market was affected by the strange music.

Mr Wobbly Man rocked gently and dreamily from side to side. Clockwork Mouse swirled round and round. Clockwork Clown performed slow, lazy somersaults.

They were all snapped out of their dream-like dances as the record suddenly stopped.

"Very strange music!" exclaimed Sammy Sailor. "What is it?"

Big-Ears explained that the sound was a recording of the Singing Bush. "It's a magical thing," he told them, "in a secret spot – deep, deep in the wood!"

"Did you see all that, Sly?" Gobbo whispered in astonishment as they secretly watched everyone at the market.

"It strikes me that folk would pay a lot of sixpences to dance along to the Singing Bush! If only we could find out where that secret spot is..."

"What joy to hear the Singing Bush again!" Big-Ears remarked to himself merrily as he made his way home. "Such delicate music!"

Little did Big-Ears realise that the two goblins were lying in wait for him!

"We'll capture Big-Ears in my fishing net!" chuckled
Gobbo.

"Help! Help!" Big-Ears cried as a net suddenly
dropped on top of him. "I'm all tangled up!"

"So it's you two wicked goblins who set this trap for me!"
Big-Ears exclaimed as Sly and Gobbo gleefully
surrounded him. "Let me out at once!"

"No, we won't!" Gobbo replied firmly. "Not until you
have taken us to the Singing Bush!"

Noddy also happened to be in the wood. He had finished polishing his car and was driving it to Big-Ears' house to show him how shiny it was.

By chance, he noticed Big-Ears' bicycle lying on the ground. "Why has he left it here?" he said to himself, starting to become rather worried.

Soon afterwards, Noddy heard someone crying for help through the trees. He quickly followed the cries, certain they were from Big-Ears.

Noddy gasped on finding Big-Ears trapped in the goblins' net.

"Go for help!" Big-Ears ordered him urgently. "Fetch Mr Plod!"

Just as Noddy was hurrying away, Gobbo cast a wicked spell on him.

"It's called my Runaway Spell!" he sniggered to Sly. "Now no one will be friendly to Noddy. No one will help him. They'll just want to run away from him!"

Noddy soon reached his car and jumped in. "We must hurry and fetch Mr Plod!" he cried. But his car hurled him straight out again and sped away.

The goblins' wicked Runaway Spell was working already!

Noddy had to make his way to Toy Town on foot and so it was quite a time before he reached Mr Plod's police station.

"Mr Plod!" Noddy gasped breathlessly. "There you are! I need help!"

"You should have thought of that before you got up this morning!" Mr Plod snapped. And he walked straight out the door, not helping Noddy at all!

It seemed that no one would help poor Noddy. Not even Tessie Bear!

"Tessie, I'm so glad you've come to see me!" he said joyfully when he met her outside his house.

"I haven't!" she replied sharply. "Why should I have tea with a silly wooden doll like you!"

Noddy was so upset. He just could not understand why all his friends were being so horrible.

Then he suddenly realised. The goblins must have put a wicked spell on him so everyone would avoid him!

"I'll just have to help Big-Ears on my own!" Noddy said to himself bravely as he headed into the Dark Wood, plunging through the trees.

By now it was getting dark and the wood was becoming more and more eerie.

Before long, Noddy had become well and truly lost!

"I've never been to this part of the wood before!" he said to himself nervously.

Noddy heard distant voices and looked up. He could just make out some torch lights flashing as well!

"What's that?" he whispered. "Big-Ears? The goblins?"

Noddy crept carefully towards the torch lights but suddenly a twig cracked under his foot.

"What's that?" snapped Sly, shining his torch directly at him.

"Noddy!" Big-Ears declared joyfully. "I'm delighted to see you!"

"What! He shouldn't be delighted to see Noddy!" Gobbo exclaimed crossly.

Fearing that the Runaway Spell was wearing off, Gobbo ordered Sly to cast a new one on Noddy.

Then the strangest thing happened – Sly became very
friendly!

"Noddy! How kind of you to come all this way on
such a dark night!" he said, shaking his hand.

Meanwhile, Gobbo started to help Big-Ears out of the
net. "Come on Big-Ears, out of that net!" he told
him kindly.

Gobbo's kindness did not last very long, however.

"What are we doing?" he exclaimed to himself suddenly. "I shouldn't be helping people!"

"This is all your fault!" Gobbo shouted at Sly. "You cast that Runaway Spell with your left hand instead of your right hand! It's working backwards! Now everyone wants to be with Noddy!"

Seeing Mr Plod approach in Noddy's car, Gobbo and Sly both fled into the darkness!

Tessie Bear was also in Noddy's car and this time she was as happy to see Noddy as he was to see her!

"I'm afraid the goblins have run off," Big-Ears told Mr Plod. "They've done no real harm. After all, they'll miss what they really wanted..."

"Where is the Singing Bush?" Noddy asked curiously.

At that very moment, a delicate magical music engulfed them. They all started to dance and twirl dreamily.

"Here it is!" Big-Ears told them all softly. "The goblins don't know it but the Singing Bush was right next to me all the time!"

"We must let it be," Big-Ears added in a gentle whisper. "Come to my Toadstool House for cocoa..."

So the toys all tip-toed away from the Singing Bush, leaving it to make its strange delicate music in the moonlight.

And that was the last any of them would see of it.

When morning came, the bush would look just like any other in the wood so that no one could ever steal its magic...

This edition first published in Great Britain by HarperCollins Publishers Ltd in 2000

1 3 5 7 9 10 8 6 4 2

Copyright © 1999 Enid Blyton Ltd. Enid Blyton's signature mark and the words
"NODDY" and "TOYLAND" are Registered Trade Marks of Enid Blyton Ltd.
For further information on Enid Blyton please contact www.blyton.com

ISBN: 0 00 136176 7

Reproduction by Graphic Studio S.r.l. Verona
Printed in Italy by Garzanti Verga S.r.l.

MORE NODDY BOOKS FOR YOU TO ENJOY

Noddy and the Artists

Noddy and the Bouncing Ball

Noddy and the Goblins

Noddy Tidies Toyland

Noddy and the Treasure Map

Noddy and the Noisy Drum

Noddy is Caught in a Storm

Noddy and the Driving Lesson

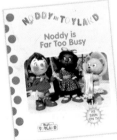

Noddy is Far Too Busy

Noddy and the Magic Watch

Noddy the Nurse

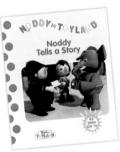

Noddy Tells a Story